# PRAISE FOR
# THE WHALE CHILD

"The story guides the reader using traditional Coast Salish lore in a contemporary narrative, masterfully weaving the timeless wisdom of Indigenous ways of knowing into our current reality."

—**SHERRI MITCHELL WEH'NA HA'MU KWASSET,** author of *Sacred Instructions*

"*The Whale Child* provides that 'smart step in the right direction' we all need."

—**PAUL OWEN LEWIS,** author and illustrator of *Storm Boy* and *Frog Girl*

"*The Whale Child* is an environmental fable for our time. . . . at turns educational, poignant, warm, sad, and funny. . . . an important book for children, parents, and teachers to read and ponder."

—**BRYN BARNARD,** author of *The New Ocean*

"A long time ago, we didn't have to be taught that everything has a spirit, a life force, a memory, a moment that all things came into existence. . . . Brother and sister Keith and Chenoa Egawa bring us back to those teachings in their story *The Whale Child*. . . . We learn how to quiet our minds to hear the message that Mother Earth holds the cure, the answers, and the way to heal her if we just take a moment to reconnect and hear what she has to say."

—**JANINE GIBBONS,** Haida artist and children's book illustrator for the *Baby Raven Reads* series, Sealaska Heritage Institute

"The critical insights of our responsibilities and the truth of reciprocity— particularly with water, the first medicine—are woven into each page. Through playful adventure, the essence of ancient instructions emerges in the context of a modern world."

—**VALERIE SEGREST,** Muckleshoot, author, Native food systems strategist, and wild medicine expert

"This magical tale of a whale child, coming to shore as a boy to show a young Coastal Salish girl the terrible effects of pollution on the water cycle, reads almost like a parable. Its gentle tone and added humor guide us to understand how all life is interconnected, from water bugs to whales."

—**KEELY PARRACK,** author of *Morning, Sunshine!*

# -THE-
# WHALE
# CHILD

# -THE-
# WHALE CHILD

KEITH EGAWA

-AND-

CHENOA EGAWA

North Atlantic Books
Berkeley, California

Published by North Atlantic Books
Berkeley, California

Cover art by Keith Egawa and Chenoa Egawa
Cover design by Jasmine Hromjak
Book design by Happenstance Type-O-Rama

Printed in Canada

*The Whale Child* is sponsored and published by the Society for the Study of Native Arts and Sciences (dba North Atlantic Books), an educational nonprofit based in Berkeley, California, that collaborates with partners to develop cross-cultural perspectives, nurture holistic views of art, science, the humanities, and healing, and seed personal and global transformation by publishing work on the relationship of body, spirit, and nature.

North Atlantic Books' publications are available through most bookstores. For further information, visit our website at www.northatlanticbooks.com or call 800-733-3000.

Library of Congress Cataloging-in-Publication Data
Names: Egawa, Keith, 1966- author. | Egawa, Chenoa, author.
Title: The whale child / Keith Egawa and Chenoa Egawa.
Description: Berkeley, California : North Atlantic Books, [2020] | Includes
    bibliographical references. | Summary: Shiny, a whale child, is turned
    into a boy to teach Alex, a young girl, the wisdom of the Native
    American value of environmental stewardship so that she can share it
    with others. Includes glossary of environmental terms, facts about
    Pacific Northwest Native cultures, and other educational resources.
Identifiers: LCCN 2020005264 (print) | LCCN 2020005265 (ebook) | ISBN
    9781623174866 (trade paperback) | ISBN 9781623174873 (ebook)
Subjects: CYAC: Environmental protection—Fiction. | Water—Fiction. |
    Coast Salish Indians—Fiction. | Indians of North America—Washington
    (State)—Fiction. | Whales—Fiction. | Magic—Fiction.
Classification: LCC PZ7.1.E2955 Wh 2020  (print) | LCC PZ7.1.E2955  (ebook)
    | DDC [Fic]—dc23
LC record available at https://lccn.loc.gov/2020005264
LC ebook record available at https://lccn.loc.gov/2020005265

1 2 3 4 5 6 7 8 9 FRIESENS 25 24 23 22 21 20

This book includes recycled material and material from well-managed forests. North Atlantic Books is committed to the protection of our environment. We print on recycled paper whenever possible and partner with printers who strive to use environmentally responsible practices.

FOR OUR WHALE CHILD—
CREA TAIMANEIMOANA;
FOR ALEX, BELLA, AND ELIANA,
AND FOR ALL THE CHILDREN OF THE WORLD.
MAY THEIR LOVE, CARE, HONESTY,
AND COURAGE ENSURE A FUTURE
IN HARMONY AND BALANCE
WITH OUR MOTHER EARTH.

# Chapter 1

In our world today there lives a whale child, born not so long ago in the waters of the South Pacific Ocean. You may have seen him from the shore, off in the distance, swimming with his mother. Like all children, he came into the world with kindness in his soul, an eagerness to learn, and the open mind of a newborn. He arrived with the strength of all the ancestors who came before him, and many other gifts yet to be realized.

His name arose from the movements of the great sea and the light reaching down through the water, sparkling beneath the waves, though it is a name that cannot be pronounced with our human voices. Sunlight dances, shines, and shimmers upon the water's surface as the whale child passes, and when he is close, the countless creatures of the world's oceans feel hope within the currents made by the movements of his fins. And they all sense he is special. Bright light twinkles within the inky blackness of the whale child's eyes, as if the stars came down from their home in the night sky to rest there in his gentle gaze.

From the earliest days of his life, the whale child's mother taught him the language of the sea through timeless songs that carry the stories and wisdom of life on earth. She told him how water is the source of life.

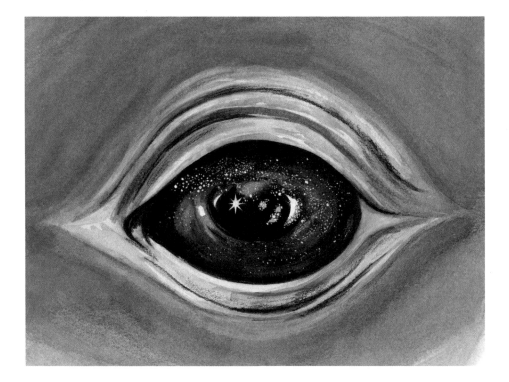

Not only the dark and salty water of their ocean home, but the water that flows sweet and clear over the land; the water that sits in still lakes, ponds, and marshes; and the water that falls down to us from the sky . . . all of these many pathways joining together to create the living veins of our planet.

"Listen and remember," said the whale child's mother. "The earth's waters are sacred, as all living things must have water to survive. Listen and remember . . . all creatures of the ocean were healthy and strong, back when clean waters could carry a song to the ears of others far away in bountiful oceans through dark night and bright day. But now I will show you things that are happening in the sea and on land. And you my child . . . you will share what you learn."

The whale child remained with his mother in the warm southern waters of his birth until he had built up plenty of insulating fat for the icy Arctic. Then his mother led him on the long journey north, and there they spent the spring and summer months in the cold northern waters, swimming along the coastline by glaciers and sea ice. There they fed on small fish, plankton, and tiny shrimp called krill that appeared within the ocean in groups as large and numerous as clouds in the sky. She taught her child to swim straight up toward the surface beneath the swirling schools of krill, using the brushy filters that whales have in their mouths, called baleen, to filter the tiny creatures from the water. She also taught him to stay clear of ships and boats that could strike and kill a whale. She taught him to recognize and avoid fishing nets that could entangle a whale's body and fins. At all times she kept her baby close by her side, often reaching out and touching him with a giant flipper to make sure he was close and protected.

To the whale child, the beauty and abundance of his world were endless as he glided through the water, never far from the protective shadow of his mother. He was safe and happy, and he would show his joy in the same way he'd seen his mother and other whales do, by launching himself clear of the surface and crashing back down with enormous, thunderous splashes.

The whale child and his mother traveled great distances, following their migratory paths, back and forth between the warm blue waters nearer the equator and those that were dark green and very cold farther north. Along the way, his mother began showing him things happening to their ocean world because of the people who lived on the land. Along the way, she showed him how things were changing.

One evening, off the coast of the Pacific Northwest, a pod of orcas passed with soundless speed, racing smoothly toward the next hunting ground. And here, not far from shore, the whale child and his mother decided to rest for the night. And it was here that the whale child

asked his mother, "What things have I learned? What things will I share?"

"Do you know how to survive?" his mother answered. "And do you know what things you need in order to continue surviving? Do you remember all that you've seen on our travels?"

"Yes," nodded the whale child.

"Then you also know what all other living things need to survive. And there is more you know that you have not yet considered or remembered."

As the mother and her child floated peacefully at the surface resting from their travels, the whale child dreamed. In his dream, the moonlight reached down into the deep ocean, and he saw a human woman in the distance swimming toward him. Her long dark hair flowed out behind her and rippled in the current like smooth black seaweed.

The whale child knew this was more than a dream. He knew that it was showing him what was to come. He did not yet know how or why, but he knew this woman would soon welcome him onto the shore of the human world.

When his mother awoke, she confided, "I had the same dream as you, and what you dreamed was true. You have family on land as you do in the sea. We are all connected . . . we are all related. Now, my son, you will walk on two feet as men do, and you will meet a woman and her daughter where the surf meets the sand. The woman is your human mother. The little girl is your human sister.

"To this little girl you will pass on our teachings, and by helping her, she will in turn help others bring healing to the world. As tomorrow's sun rises, you will emerge from the sea as a human boy, and you will show your little sister that being a caretaker of the earth begins with taking care of the water that all life depends on. Your visit on land will be very short, but during the quickly passing time, you will

show her that she can help overcome the things you and I have seen in our travels . . . one smart step at a time."

"But that seems impossible," marveled the whale child.

His mother made a slight movement of her powerful fin, drifting closer until her eye was right next to his. "Now listen carefully," she said. "The spirit of the ocean moves within every drop of water, traveling the globe within the largest and smallest of currents. It lives within the bubbling, roiling waves, within the seafoam on the still surface, and down into the deepest trenches carved in the ocean floor. This spirit has been with us and around us since the beginning of all things, and during every part of your travels by my side. It has witnessed your happiness and your reactions to the bad things you have seen, when you looked upon the many threats to life in the ocean. It has seen that you are not disheartened and do not give up in the face of difficulty and challenge. So, of all the creatures of the ocean, the water spirit has chosen you for what will happen next. It has chosen you to carry the wisdom and memory, not only of all the whales who came before you, but the wisdom and memory of the vast ocean world and its connections to life on dry land. It has chosen you to share this wisdom with the humans, who will be responsible for what happens to the earth. The spirit of the ocean knows that you are perfect for the task at hand."

Before the whale child could ask his mother more about what all of this meant, the tiny bioluminescent lights that glitter throughout the ocean gathered around him. The water swirled and churned, forming the shape of the water spirit. And as the whale child watched in amazement, the water spirit reached out with a long arm of seawater and starlight, and gently touched him on the top of his head.

Then the whale child began to change. He shrank and grew skinny as his thick hide became thin. The deep gray of his body faded, until soon he was the color of the humans on the shore, and his skin reflected the lights that swirled around him, making him glow within the deep shadows of the ocean, like the lure of an angler fish. His fins became arms, and where his powerful tail had been, there were now two human legs, kicking to keep his new body afloat. His eyes moved forward from the sides of his head, and soon he was looking toward the beach where the humans lived. Then the water spirit disappeared. The water became dark and calm again, and the whale child was a boy paddling about in the deep ocean.

"Go ashore now, my son," the mother whale pressed, fondly. "They are expecting you. Take with you all of my love and confidence, and I will remain out here to watch over you from the bay."

At that, the boy swam toward the shore, and each time he poked his head up from the water he could see the hulking shapes of hills and mountains in the distance, growing closer. When the water was nearly shallow enough for him to stand, he ran face-first into a pair of old surf shorts floating on the surface.

"I guess this is lucky," he thought aloud. "A human losing his shorts in the ocean and me finding them." He had seen people before, and the clothing they put on their bodies. So, for the first time, he stood on his new legs. "How strange is this?" he muttered, as he awkwardly climbed into the shorts, one leg and then the other, feeling the gritty sand against his feet and between his toes.

Although he could wade the rest of the distance to the beach, he slipped back beneath the surface and swam forward, feeling the weight of the unknown upon him.

But the comfort of his mother's love remained strong and steady within each beat of his heart as he made his way through the push and pull of the shifting tides. And he was not afraid.

# CHAPTER 2

A little girl named Alex lived a content and happy life in the Pacific Northwest, close to the seashore with her mother and father. It was a place of tall green trees and water all around. Her mother's people were called Coast Salish, and they had lived in this place further back than history could remember. Her father's people were Polynesian, and they came from a distant island in the South Pacific Ocean. Both sides of Alex's family had important ties to the land and sea. Her great-grandparents, and the generations before them, knew that living in harmony with nature would ensure a healthy and plentiful world for the children yet to come. But, when Alex was born, the respect and understanding that her ancestors held dear needed to be remembered by the living. Alex's mind was as sharp as a little fishhook, but she had not yet thought about things that might be wrong with her world and the future.

One night, Alex's mother had a dream. In this dream, she swam out into the ocean toward a mother whale and her baby. In her dream, the baby whale turned into a human boy and she welcomed him ashore. From her dream, she knew that this boy would share important gifts with her daughter. She knew that Alex would truly listen and understand. She knew Alex would share what she learned with a waiting world of young minds and open ears.

When she awoke, she walked down to her daughter's room. As it was a summer night, it was still hot inside the house. Alex had slid out of bed in her sleep to escape the heat of her blankets, so she was

splayed on the rug like an exhausted lizard. In one hand she held a stuffed sheep named Sheepy, and in the other she clutched a half-eaten doughnut she'd sneaked during the night. "Wake up, Alex." Her mother shook her gently. "There's something we must go see." And she walked her daughter down to the beach in the dark.

As the sun rose from behind the mountains to the east, Alex and her mother stood side by side watching the changing colors of dawn light up the surf that rolled back and forth upon the glistening sand.

Alex looked out toward the horizon and believed she saw two whale tails in the distance, one big and one small, breaking the surface and then disappearing. Then Alex heard the haunting notes of a whale song drifting in on the tide. The song gradually grew louder then stopped, and as she and her mother watched and waited, a human boy came up from the ocean.

"Who is that?" Alex asked.

"He is the boy I dreamed of," her mother answered. "He is your brother from the water . . . the boy who comes from the whales."

Alex knew whales held a special place in the stories and legends of both her mother's and father's people. Elders called them *the people who live under the water,* and they represented the strength of community and working together. They could inspire happiness and luck, and she even heard that sometimes the presence of a whale meant that you were protected on your travels. But still, her mother's words were hard to believe.

"My brother from the whales?" blurted Alex. "But that seems impossible! He must be a boy who fell off a boat or went for a late-night swim and lost his way . . . swept down the shoreline by a riptide."

As Alex's mother watched the boy make his way toward them, she too was astounded by what she saw. But in a calm voice she said to her little girl, "Magic such as this has always existed in the world, and nature will now teach you ancient and eternal truths for a better future. This boy is here to share lessons with a child of pure heart and open mind. So, you must listen closely to what he says . . . for that special child is you, and his visit will pass quickly."

Alex felt the truth of this, and her disbelief faded. She nodded and approached the boy with the comfort and kindness that children are born with and adults often forget. "What's your name?" she asked.

The boy spat out a big mouthful of water, seaweed, and sand. He blinked his eyes then said, "Do you know how the sunlight shines on the waves when you look out over the ocean?"

"Yes," said Alex. "I know it well."

"Well, in my language . . . the language of the sea . . . my name means *sunlight that shines into the deep ocean.*"

"That's a very long name. I will call you Shiny," declared Alex.

To that, the boy nodded his head and smiled, showing big chunks of green seaweed still stuck in his front teeth.

"So you are a . . ."

" . . . yup . . . a whale," Shiny confirmed.

Alex nodded slowly, her eyes wide and the beginnings of a smile on her lips. "But that seems . . ."

"Impossible?" said Shiny.

"Yup. Seems impossible."

Shiny looked back over his shoulder. "But here I am." He gestured toward the ocean. "And I came from far out there."

Alex thought about her mother's words of magic in the world, and this *was* happening before her very eyes after all. So, Alex replied, "Oh, I believe it. I said it *seems* impossible . . . not that it *is* impossible. And here you are, and here we are together."

Just then, a small shape appeared in the sky above their heads. It moved from inland, heading toward the sea, and Alex flinched when

18

the winged shadow dove down toward them before gliding out over the bay. The silhouette quacked loudly, with a croak like a toad with a frog in its throat, and Alex realized it was a duck, already awake and on the wing.

"Go find a nice little pond to float in," she called out to the bird, "before you crash into the ocean and get swallowed by a goosefish!"

Shiny smiled and nodded his head, but said nothing as he watched the duck pass by.

# CHAPTER 3

Shiny slept for a while, snoring and gurgling like a walrus with a bad cold. When he awoke later that morning, he found that Alex had not gone back to sleep, and she was instead patiently watching and waiting for him to get up. She had retrieved some clothes from one of her older cousins, and they were in a neatly folded pile at Shiny's feet, so that he could choose from the stack of hand-me-downs.

"How are you feeling?" she asked.

"A little odd, to be honest," said Shiny.

"That's understandable," acknowledged Alex. "After all, you did lose over a thousand pounds since yesterday. Probably not easy to adjust to such sudden skinniness."

Shiny held his thin arms out in front of him and wiggled his ten fingers like a nest of restless bugs. "Yes. A drastic difference indeed."

Alex led Shiny to her thinking tree, where she often sat and looked out over the ocean, thinking thoughts of yesterday, today, and tomorrow.

"So, tell me about your visit," said Alex. "Mom says you have important teachings to share in a very short time."

"Ah yes . . . ," said Shiny, "teachings about water and how all life depends on it. I will show you the paths that water follows."

"The paths?" wondered Alex. "What paths?"

Shiny considered her question, then asked, "Where does your drinking water come from, Alex?"

"Straight out of the faucet," she replied.

Shiny laughed. "There's much more to it than that. Listen . . . the rain comes down and goes into the ground. It sits in pools and lakes. And way up high, to nearly the sky, huge glaciers water makes. It freezes, it melts, it evaporates, and up in the clouds it waits."

"Hmmm," Alex pondered. "Not sure what that's all about. I think you better show me."

"That's the plan," said Shiny. "And I will show you how people are interrupting and destroying these paths. These things are there for everyone to see, but seeing doesn't seem to be enough."

"Enough for what?" asked Alex.

"Enough to make humans change their behavior and not take the health of water for granted."

"Okay then, my brother from the sea," said Alex. "Let's go see these teachings."

From the moment Shiny had stepped onto the beach and stood before her, Alex felt comfort in his presence, despite the unusual nature of his arrival and the uncertainty of what lay ahead. She felt safe and at peace when Shiny stood close by.

"Come along with me," said Shiny, "and I will show you."

At the edge of the village, Alex paused in an open space on the outskirts of the forest. She listened and she waited.

Shiny pointed in all directions. "Ah, the natural world . . . ," he marveled. "Creatures and spirits and fantastic forces unseen. It may

seem as simple and familiar as the rock and the tree but it is full of powerful mystery."

"Like magic," said Alex.

"Yes, exactly that," said Shiny. "Now, let your mind be silent and still as you listen and learn . . . let your heart be open. The natural world is alive, beautiful, and giving. But it can be lost when people do not take care of it. I will show you how things are changing in very bad ways."

"I don't believe I'd like to see those things." Alex shuddered.

And to this, Shiny answered, "In the time we're now living you have no choice but to see them, because to ignore these difficult things is to let them keep happening."

Shiny saw that Alex looked dismayed at the thought of losing her beautiful and giving world. So, he put his hand on her shoulder. "Do not lose hope," he added. "Seeing what is bad will make you realize the good you can do. Take one smart step in the right direction and the next will come much easier."

Just then, a little duck with an extra-large head landed next to them on the grass. He stretched his short wings and squawked loudly. Then he pecked at Alex's foot, his beak making thumping noises against her rubber boot.

"Hey . . . I know that croak in my bones!" exclaimed Alex. "You're the duck who flew over our heads this morning on the beach."

The duck quacked again, to which Shiny answered, "Yes, of course. Come along with us and help bring the world into view. Bufflehead, meet Alex. And Alex, meet Bufflehead. And Bufflehead, stop chewing on her boot."

Alex frowned and looked doubtfully at the bold little bird. But she said nothing and followed Shiny.

# Chapter 4

Shiny and Alex quickly became friends. And as they traveled the countryside, through grassy fields and shady forests, it was as though they had always known one another.

When midday arrived, they stopped on a sandy beach to rest. Alex found a log where a brown lizard was sunning himself, and she sat down and emptied her lunch bag. She set aside a little cupcake with blue frosting and ate a cheese sandwich and an apple. But since Shiny was still a whale at heart, he dove back into the ocean, chasing after shrimp and small fish. Alex watched him slipping and darting within the waves, and when she noticed Bufflehead next to her, she gave him a crust from her sandwich. "Eat up, Buffley. And don't sit on that little reptile creeping down the log."

Alex noticed that Bufflehead ignored the lizard and kept his head cocked sideways, with his little black eye focused on her. So, she concentrated to see if she too could make him speak so that she could understand, as Shiny seemed to do. But no words or sounds came from the duck.

Once Shiny had gotten his fill, he came out of the water and walked up to the log where Alex and Bufflehead waited.

"That's a lot of strong-smelling sea life you just ate out there," said Alex. "Do whale boys brush their teeth?"

"Whales don't and boys do," said Shiny. "So, I guess whale boys are a little confused about it."

Alex had taken a few steps down toward the shore to look out over the ocean, and now she turned away from the water to look back at Shiny. "Did you just eat my cupcake?" she asked.

"No."

"Then how come your mouth is all blue?"

Shiny laughed and shook his hair dry like a dog. "I'm sorry, I had to test it," he said, "to see what kinds of food you humans are eating."

Then his face grew serious, as he looked slowly up and down the shoreline. "Look there on the beach, Alex. Fish and birds get tangled in nets that are left to drift. Some have eaten garbage and died. Even the small things that people toss to the ground, here and there without thinking, add up to very big problems. Did you know most of the plastic that's made, used, and then thrown away by humans ends up in the sea?

"Thousands and thousands of heaps and piles and miles . . . tons and tons of plastic garbage . . . out there choking the world's oceans. I have seen it myself. I swam through it, around it, and beneath it while traveling with my mother."

Alex looked down the beach and saw dead fish and birds scattered across the sand. She could see the pieces of plastic they had eaten. She saw a bird that had become entangled in nets. She saw a crab with his claw caught in a plastic soda pop ring. She looked out toward the waves and saw more litter floating and bobbing in the shallows.

"I'm sorry to show you such sad, frightening things," mumbled Shiny. "Being here with you is more fun than I could have known, but I was allowed this visit because the world has become such a dangerous place. Remember what I said earlier. If we do not learn about everything we face in life—both good and bad, light and dark—then we are ignoring the truth. To look at the world honestly is to see the difficulty that is there."

Alex nodded and sighed heavily. But she still had a frown on her face. Shiny stepped forward to look her in the eye. "Alex, we don't stop laughing just because there is bad in the world. And we don't ignore the bad so that we can keep laughing. And Alex . . . never stop enjoying the blue cupcakes."

"You mean enjoy the cupcakes when a whale boy doesn't eat them first?"

Both kids laughed loudly, and the sound could be heard in all directions, far down the beach and out over the ocean.

Now with a smile on her face, Alex said, "I'm okay, cupcake thief. Let's see something else."

Shiny and Alex followed along the water's edge, and later that afternoon they came to a still inlet where the mouth of a river emptied into the ocean. Here there were no houses.

They arrived at a point where a dark oily liquid gushed forth from two big metal pipes jutting out from a concrete wall. "Look here." Shiny pointed down. "Pollution that flows and grows until the creatures of the ocean can no longer live in it."

"Yes," nodded Alex. "I've seen these pipes and the yucky glop they gush all day. Definitely stinky, my friend . . . very stinky."

"They are everywhere," said Shiny. "Not just here, but near and far. Pipes and pollution crossing the planet." Then Shiny thought about the water spirit that had formed before his eyes, changing him and making his visit on land possible. "And remember . . . ," he said, "water is alive. Water is life for each living thing from the smallest to the biggest, from tardigrades to blue whales . . . from eels to elephants. So, imagine what happens as their world is poisoned."

"That is a very serious problem. What's a tardigrade?"

"The water bear," explained Shiny, "a creature too tiny for the human eye to find."

Alex imagined a brown bear with claws, teeth, and hackles, but so itsy-bitsy it could swim laps in a bottle cap. "Pretty neat," she said. "Grizzly bears paddling around in a drop of water. I like the sound of it."

Shiny smiled and took a few steps, preparing to continue their journey. But Alex lingered for a moment longer, thinking. "Protect them all, from the big to the small," she announced to the clouds overhead. Then she looked back at the pipes pumping pollution. "My parents told me that their grandparents, great-grandparents, and those far back before them all lived by the understanding that every speck of life helps hold our world together."

"Yes," said Shiny. "People know this, but then it's forgotten. Forgotten and remembered. Remembered and forgotten."

"I'm beginning to see that," said Alex. "So, this is a time for remembering."

# Chapter 5

"Let's head to the mouth of that river," said Shiny, "and from there we'll walk inland." The two friends left the shore behind them, plodding their way through thick brush as high as Alex's shoulders. Soon the ground before them opened into an expanse of gray sand and pebbles, with larger rocks and boulders dotting both banks of the river. The kids followed its path as it curved back and forth like a gigantic crawling snake. Now they were miles inland, alone in the deep, still silence, except for the soft sound and movement of the river flowing out from a wall of cedar and fir trees that covered the land sloping gradually up toward the mountains.

"I know this river well," Alex noted. "It moves slowly here, but a little way up ahead into the trees the water begins to crash and tumble with current so powerful it can sweep a kid away like a piece of driftwood. The salmon that my people have always depended on come up this river to spawn every year, fighting their way through the wildest waters. Then their eggs hatch, new salmon are born, and they head out to sea to grow and live their lives. Then, as adults they come back here again to spawn. In fact . . . look there, Shiny!"

Alex pointed into the clear, sparkling water, where a small group of salmon pushed against the current, around and over the slippery brown rocks that stuck up above the water line.

"Ah yes," said Shiny. "We're thinking the same now, Alex! Salmon are just what I hoped to see!"

"This is something I know a lot about," reported Alex. "Salmon have been the most important food source for my people since . . . well, forever. We are called *the people of the salmon,* and we could not have survived without these fish. The stories say that long ago, the salmon made an agreement with the people of the land. They would return to the rivers each year to feed the people. But only if humans continued to honor them, giving thanks and showing their gratitude by ensuring the salmons' habitat was kept clean and healthy. They would always return if people took only what was needed, so that the salmon would thrive forever. In my great-grandparents' time, the returning salmon were so plentiful they say you could walk across the river on their backs. But now their numbers are small . . . a tiny fraction of what used to be."

"Yes," said Shiny, "I have seen them in the ocean, swift and powerful adult salmon moving through the deep, like streaks of silver light.

My mother told me that they used to be huge, nearly twice the size of the ones I have seen in my short lifetime."

"Right," said Alex. "My mom showed me old photos of my ancestors standing next to wooden racks of harvested salmon, and the fish were bigger than me. Shiny, what's going on here? What is happening to the salmon?"

Bufflehead coasted in from the cedar trees and pulled up fast a foot or so above the river. He held his position there for a moment, watching the salmon pass beneath him. Then he dropped to the surface with a plop, paddling his webbed feet just enough to keep from drifting downriver, back toward the ocean.

Shiny stayed silent for a bit, letting the knowledge and memory he'd been gifted by the water spirit move through his mind and body. Then he spoke. "The fish don't grow as big, and their numbers grow fewer and fewer, because of overharvesting. They're captured before they can fully grow. But there's a lot more to it than that."

Now Shiny scanned the distance and pointed down the coast to where smokestacks from a factory stood high above a distant hilltop. "Look there, Alex. See those sour, sooty fumes billowing up into the sky? Those clouds of pollution pumped into the air eventually fall to the ground, contaminating soil and water. There are pesticides used on farms that also go into the soil, then into the river, and all of this ends up in the flesh of salmon and countless other aquatic creatures."

"My family only eats salmon sparingly now," said Alex, "and my mother says it is because of the mercury in the fish."

"Yes, poison in their flesh," agreed Shiny. "And Alex, you spoke of how the salmon runs that once filled the river from shore to shore are no more. That is not only true of this river in your corner of the world; there are in fact places where no fish return at all. These are signs telling us that things have gone terribly wrong and will undoubtedly get worse. When salmon disappear from a river, this tells you the river is no longer healthy and cannot sustain life. So pay attention to the signs. Notice everything the natural world shows you. And know that what I just told you barely scratches the surface."

Before Alex could answer, there was a violent splash as a salmon broke the surface near the river's edge, its entire body rising out of the water with flashes of silver, brown, and red. The salmon plowed its way along the gravel through the shallows and nearly crashed into Bufflehead, as he bobbed peacefully on the surface. Bufflehead leaped out of the explosion of white water, away from the thrashing fish. Then, in a panic, the little duck headed straight for Alex, his wings flapping violently around her head and spraying her face in a flurry of mist and feathers.

"Yikes! You crazy bird!" Alex shouted, doubling over with laughter. "What is your deal?"

Bufflehead landed by Alex's feet, calmer now and looking almost embarrassed. He cocked his head to the side and watched the lone salmon swim out of sight on its way farther upstream.

Shiny was laughing too, wiping the tears from his eyes. Then he looked to the west, where the sun had begun its descent toward the horizon. He caught his breath. "Look, we're running out of daylight."

Alex dabbed the water off her face with her shirtsleeve. "I was thinking the same thing. In a couple hours we can be home."

"Then let's go back and sleep," suggested Shiny, "and when the sun comes up, we'll head out again."

Alex led the way, and the companions began the trek back to her house.

"Hey Alex. Did you notice that Bufflehead flew to you for protection?"

"Yes, I did. I guess I'll take that as a compliment, huh?"

The travelers arrived home as the sun was dipping down into the ocean, where somewhere Shiny's mother cruised just beneath the surface, feeling the presence of her child on the land.

# CHAPTER 6

~~~~~~~~~~~~~~~~~~~~~~~~~~~~~~~~~~~~~~~~~~~~~~~~~

The next morning, Shiny and Alex headed back in the direction that yesterday's adventure had taken them. But this time they walked much farther inland, leaving the shore far behind. They hiked through a stretch of coastal wetlands and open grassy fields, passing an empty barn used long ago by farmers.

Soon Shiny stopped and pointed to the smokestacks of the factory they had seen the day before. "Alex, look beyond those columns of pollution billowing up into the sky. Look way up to the mountains before us. Do you see the white snow on the high peaks? Do you see the glacier?"

"Yes," said Alex. "It's beautiful and pure up there."

"Beautiful, yes," said Shiny. "But let's go higher up still . . . up into the foothills. From there we may see the mountains in close and clear silence. And along the way we will see what we see and learn what is to be learned. Come along. There's more walking to do."

"But which direction . . . which route . . . which trail will take us there?" asked Alex.

Shiny looked around as if something was missing. He raised one eyebrow and then the other. "Where's Bufflehead gone off to?" he mumbled.

Just then, a flock of geese passed overhead, honking loudly.

Alex pointed skyward. "Look," she crowed. "There's Bufflehead flying with the honkers!" Hearing Alex's voice, Bufflehead broke off from the flock and dove down to flutter above the children. Then he landed in a patch of clover and scared up a bumblebee that bumped into Alex's forehead so hard it made a sound like the snapping of fingers.

Bufflehead flapped his wings and made a loud squawk.

"Yes, yes, Bufflehead," acknowledged Shiny. "That makes sense. Now, lead on."

"I have to ask . . ." Alex looked at Shiny with a quizzical eye. "Are you really speaking with that duck?"

"Of course I'm speaking with the duck." Shiny grinned. "And the duck is speaking with me."

Alex was still not entirely sure about this. But Bufflehead was a wild creature, after all, and the way he followed them so closely and without fear surely had to mean something out of the ordinary—something truly magical and no harder to accept than everything else of the past two days. So, Alex said nothing more about it and followed along.

The three companions pressed on, making their way through the silent coastal woods. Sometimes Bufflehead hovered and swooped above their heads. Sometimes he disappeared and then returned, stopping so that Shiny and Alex could catch up.

Eventually they arrived at the last town before the foothills of the mountains. Dirt paths became paved streets and storefronts, and Alex noticed for the first time that no one looked up at the sky. Instead, they bustled to and fro like

a colony of irritated ants. Cars passed by endlessly, and people moved quickly with their heads down.

Bufflehead stood on the pavement by the kids, his webbed feet surrounded by discarded food wrappers, plastic water bottles, and broken glass.

Shiny pointed to the water bottles, which were still partially full.

"Look there. No matter how much water is used, and no matter how much water is wasted, people believe there will always be enough. Look . . . they even throw water away. Remember, Alex, you are either helping or harming through every action you take. Even the smallest things you may not worry over now are affecting the world around you, like dumping out water because you're no longer thirsty. Listen and remember . . . taking care of water is taking care of life. Small steps in the right direction."

They left the town and continued toward the mountains. As they hiked upward the world grew silent, except for the sounds of birds in the trees and creatures moving unseen in the underbrush. Alex never would have ventured this far into the wilderness alone, but she was comforted by the presence of her two new friends and pressed on with confidence.

Now Shiny and Alex stood on a hilltop, with the town far behind and the wooded landscape angling upward before them. From here, the only sign of civilization was the smoking factory pipes that poked up above the trees in the distance below.

"Look there!" Shiny pointed up to where the mountaintops filled the sky before them, glistening white with snow and ice.

Alex squinted into the sun, gazing upward. "I've never seen them so close!"

Bufflehead was now resting, nestled down on a bed of moss by Alex's feet. She could see the little duck had sat on a piece of green gum back in the town, and it was stuck and melting in his tail feathers. "You sat in gum, Buffley," she said, and stooped down to gently peel off the gooey blob. "Now, tell me, Shiny . . . ," she asked, shrugging her shoulders, "what is the lesson in this place?"

Shiny thought for a moment as he stared at Bufflehead. Then, finally he began, "The lesson is not only here in the spot we're standing. Rather, it is everywhere we've been and everywhere we will go after this . . . together and on our own. Alex, do you remember

yesterday when I asked you where your drinking water comes from? Do you remember when I said, *the rain comes down and goes into the ground. It sits in pools and lakes . . . ?*"

"Yes," continued Alex, "and way up high, to nearly the sky, huge glaciers water makes. It freezes, it melts, it evaporates, and up in the clouds it waits."

"Well done," beamed Shiny.

"But what does it wait for?" asked Alex.

"Well . . . it waits to come back down as rain."

"I see!" said Alex. "Evaporation is the mist and fog, and all that good stuff. Water rises from the ground to float like invisible rivers, flowing over our heads and above the treetops. Like magical rivers in the sky."

"Yes, Alex!" Shiny clapped. "What a beautiful way to see it! And the way you see it is so—rivers in the air above. Then, as the frozen glaciers melt, that water also comes down to us in the streams and rivers. It travels many paths over and over again. It keeps people and creatures alive and thriving, as it moves constantly from place to place, but only as long as people play their part in protecting and respecting it."

Alex thought hard. "So, like those sewer pipes that belch poison out into the ocean . . . like that factory and its smokestacks down below, and the cars we passed in town . . . all the pollution that goes up into the air eventually comes back down in the rain. And the pollution that gets stuck in the snow and ice of those glaciers will also soon come rushing down to us in the rivers, into the earth and into the ocean."

"Yes," said Shiny. "That's exactly right . . . like the river where we saw the salmon yesterday. But there is more to it than that. The pollution from industry, the exhaust from cars that we passed in the town, the burning of fossil fuels all over the world . . . it is also warming the planet.

The temperature of the atmosphere and the ocean is climbing and that glacier we're admiring, and all the others like it, are melting. But the effects of a warming planet are more far reaching than that glacier disappearing. Now, do not lose hope, as I will show you more of what I mean."

"I'm counting on it."

As the children prepared to move on, a twig snapped just a little way off. Alex raised a finger to her lips. "Listen," she whispered. "Something's coming."

As Shiny, Alex, and Bufflehead stared into the deep green of the forest, Alex glimpsed movement farther up the hill. The creature's tawny fur looked golden, in contrast to the maze of grayish-brown tree trunks and green ferns, as it slipped through the tangled undergrowth, smoothly and silently as the breeze.

Alex knew what it was, even before the big cat emerged, peeking its head up from the tall grass. "Mountain lion!" she hissed.

"Here is an unexpected lesson," Shiny whispered back. "A lesson arising from a walk in the woods. The biggest animal we've seen so far."

"Yes, we have much respect for the mountain lion," squeaked Alex. "But I fear it too."

"Sure," Shiny agreed. "He has teeth, claws, strength, and speed."

"It's a *she*."

"How do you know that?"

"I just do," Alex whispered loudly, even though the mountain lion was staring straight at them.

Shiny sidestepped closer to Alex. "But despite her power, she shares the same world and the same predicament as you and I. Without a healthy environment with all she needs—water, food, forest—she is done for. Think of the salmon, and how they grow fewer all the time. Just think if they are gone forever. Imagine if the food the cougar eats is gone someday. This is one of the ways that extinction begins."

"Cougars don't eat much salmon."

"That's not the point," insisted Shiny. "What you must recognize is that all life is connected. If an animal disappears, the sadness of its loss is only a tiny piece of the story, for its disappearance from the food chain will doom those who depend on it, one species after the next."

"Yes," said Alex. "The mountain lion is in the same boat as the rest of us."

Shiny put his hand on Alex's shoulder, ready to guide her back and away to safety. But Alex didn't move.

"Now let's make sure we survive the day!" She took several steps toward the mountain lion. "Quick, Buffley! Get on top of my head!

Stand up as straight and tall as your stubbiness will allow and spread your little wings wide as they can go!"

Alex rose on her tiptoes and waved her arms, and Bufflehead flapped his way up to perch atop her head. He stretched his neck, spread his wings, and flapped them as if he'd gone mad. Shiny looked on, eyes wide and round, eyebrows raised. The big cat regarded the group curiously from where she sat on a large gray rock. She yawned so that her long red tongue lolled out between sharp white teeth. Then she turned and disappeared without a sound.

Bufflehead returned to the ground by the children's feet and preened his ruffled wing feathers. Alex looked down at the duck, and then to where the mountain lion had been. "Did you see that?!" she cheered excitedly.

"Yes, that was quite an animal!" said Shiny.

"No, I mean . . . well yeah, the cougar is amazing. But the duck . . . Bufflehead! Did you see . . . ?"

"I sure did," said Shiny. "I saw you and him both go crazy at once."

Alex laughed, proud of her quick thinking. "You discourage cougars from coming closer by making yourself as big and bad as possible. Get it?"

"I see," smiled Shiny. "Big, bad, and crazy. That makes sense."

As the kids started for home, a raindrop hit the dry dirt in front of them. Then another and another, and soon a light rain was falling.

"Oh no," sighed Alex. "Just what we need."

"Wait," said Shiny. "This is a good thing. Do you feel that?"

Both children tilted their heads back, lifting their faces to the sky. They extended their arms out to their sides with their palms turned up to catch the drops.

"I do feel it," said Alex. "A feeling of comfort, for some reason. And look at it!" Alex pointed to where each raindrop seemed to be catching the sun's light and holding it like tiny sparks. "It looks like the ocean at night," she said. "When you swirl the water with your hand."

"That's right, Little Sister," said Shiny, "like phosphorescence. It's the spirit of the water! The one who brought me here to be with you."

"And it's watching us?" said Alex.

"Yes! We're being watched over and looked out for. The water spirit is happy we are here together."

"An acknowledgment straight from nature," said Alex. "An amazing feeling."

"C'mon, Alex. Homeward!"

The kids walked in silence for nearly another mile toward home, rejuvenated and carried onward by the rain. Then finally Alex said, "I'm glad we got to see the mountain lion. How sad that such a sight may not be possible for the kids who come after us."

# CHAPTER 7

Night was on its way when Shiny and Alex arrived back at the village. From the beach, they watched together as the sun set, making a fiery orange light on the horizon before disappearing.

"What's next?" Shiny mused aloud, glancing down at Bufflehead.

"That's your job," said Alex. "Or maybe, we should ask our little duck."

Bufflehead cocked his head to one side, then rose into the air and glided out over the ocean.

"Yes! Of course," said Shiny. "Out there, Alex." And he pointed to the vast black ocean surface, where the moon reflected in a long shimmering line the color of butter. "At one time, there was more life in the ocean than you can imagine. I need to show you what's happening out there."

Alex looked at him in disbelief. "The ocean still squirms and bulges with life."

"Not like it used to," said Shiny. "Remember what we've seen and considered in these past days, and connect all those things together in your mind. Even the oceans are changing, and now there's much less life than when my mother first breached the surface as a baby. I will show you."

Alex was skeptical. "How? I'm a human, and I can't breathe down there."

"There is another way to travel," said Shiny. "The same way your mother knew that I'd be visiting you, and just as I knew you and your mother would be there to meet me on the beach."

"What are you talking about?" Alex asked.

"In sleep you can often see more than when you're awake. Your mother and I shared the same dream of my coming here to see you, traveling toward one another beneath the water. So now, you and I will sleep and share a dream of a journey into the deep."

"Like magic," said Alex.

"Yes . . . more magic." He took a deep breath and whispered, "We lose old truths while we're awake, but a little sleep is all it takes. Your thoughts in dreams bring memory back and find new truths just down the path."

That night, as they slept, Alex dreamed that she and Shiny plunged down into the shore break. She could feel the wind blowing in from across the waves, and she could smell the salt in the chill air. When she first dunked under, she felt afraid and held her breath, but soon remembered the freedom of dreams and opened her mouth to breathe. Silver bubbles shone with a light of their own, as they enveloped Alex like a storm of rising dandelion seeds. Now she felt bigger and stronger than ever, and she swam out into an enormous deep green world that grew black in the distant open ocean, where the shapes and shadows of fish moved like ghosts through the depths.

They swam together with the skill and ease of whales, and Shiny showed Alex the things his mother had shown him. They moved past places where the currents carried harmful pollution, tangled fishing nets, and more garbage than Alex had ever seen, drifting on the surface. Alex saw an octopus crawling along the bottom, slow and smooth like a spilled milkshake spreading across the ground. But when the octopus saw the two kids swimming toward him, he quickly disappeared into an old tire.

"Alex, look there," said Shiny, pointing to the surface.

When Alex looked up, she saw an avalanche of dead sea-creatures, pouring down in the wake of a black ship, their bodies drifting and sinking toward the depths.

"What is this?" she asked.

"Overfishing," Shiny told her. "People taking too much. And they only want one type of fish, so the others caught in the net die on the deck and are dumped overboard in numbers you can't even imagine. In the last year my mother and I have seen sharks by the millions, dead and discarded with only their dorsal fins cut off so humans can make soup out of them."

At that moment Alex remembered the voices of her older relatives saying *take only what you need from nature; waste nothing and give thanks for what you take.* And at that moment she realized that there were others who might not share this belief.

She heard Shiny speak. "Get ready to make a jump many miles from here to the tropics, close to where I was born. To the South Pacific, Alex, where your father's people are from."

Alex's vision became cloudy as they moved through the ocean world in a sudden blur of shifting darkness, shadow, and moonlight.

Soon Shiny and Alex found themselves in a place where the water was much warmer. It was a lonely place where the ocean had become silent and still . . . where no creatures moved about in the miles and miles of dying coral reef.

"Look here," said Shiny. "Do you remember the pollution in the air . . . in the rain . . . in the snow and in the glaciers?"

Alex nodded. "The pollution that comes back down and flows out into the sea."

Shiny pointed to the reef. "This is what comes of that. Toxins and acid in the water destroy life in the sea, bit by bit, mile by mile, ocean by ocean. And remember when I told you of temperatures rising on the earth and in the sea? Well, this warming of the water kills the algae that nourish the coral reefs. As you see, the coral bleaches, turns white, and it dies."

Alex saw that in all directions the bare coral was a sickly greenish-brown and in places as white as bone. She saw no signs of life, except for a lone mantis shrimp walking along the bottom, searching for food that was no longer there.

"Here is another example of extinction beginning," said Shiny. "It is happening now . . . on land and in the water. Thousands of species dying off every year."

The sadness Alex felt came not only from within her heart, but now seemed to be rushing toward her from every direction and closing in on all sides, invisible but as real as the water itself. As she floated

weightless, she was struck by the clarity of the lesson. Life in the ocean would not be able to adapt to sudden changes, like a rise in temperature, even if only by a few degrees. She knew that she might see the terrible effects of this disruption in her lifetime.

Shiny turned to Alex. "Take us to the far north, where my mother and I go to feed in the summers. Take us to the Arctic."

"How?" asked Alex. "I don't even know where that is."

"You're partway in the dream world and partway out. Use your mind. See what I've seen. See what I know."

Alex relaxed and emptied her mind, no longer looking upon the dying reef. And soon she could see and feel the pathways Shiny and his mother used to travel north. Up ahead, shafts of moonlight pierced into the vast blackness of ocean that stretched as far as she could see. The temperature dropped drastically, and although Alex felt a powerful cold pressing in around her, she was not bothered by it. Soon she began to see huge shapes in the water, glowing white within the gloom.

"That is sea ice," said Shiny. "The great ice caps that cover the north and south poles of the earth, as big as mountains. But as the world grows warmer, you can watch the ice melting . . . more disappearing each year."

Shiny pointed to a huge reddish cloud, moving to and fro like the enormous flocks of starlings Alex had seen on land. "Those are krill.

My mother and I come here to eat them. Their place is down around the bottom of the food chain. That means they are part of the foundation of life. They are one of several tiny lifeforms that feed the ocean. The krill eat algae that live on and under the ice. With less ice, there are less krill, and when the ice is gone, they will be no more. So without ice there will be no life in this place."

Alex suddenly felt fear and sorrow emanating from her friend. And as she looked upon his vast and silent world and listened to his words, she knew that he was both brave and afraid.

Then her vision clouded again. The images of the ocean around her faded, as she slowly slipped from the dream world back to waking life. When she opened her eyes and saw clearly again, she was safe at home in her own bed.

# CHAPTER 8

The sun was up when Alex walked down to the beach. There she found Shiny sleeping in the surf, bobbing comfortably where the waves broke against the yellow-brown sand, and this made her smile. "My brother is still a whale at heart," she whispered to herself.

As she waded up to her ankles and called out to Shiny, she was thinking about the things she had seen . . . truths about the world that other people didn't seem to think about or know how to change. It seemed to her as though, maybe, people didn't care at all.

Shiny spat out a mouthful of seaweed, sand, and saltwater, just as he'd done the first morning they met. "And good morning to you," said Alex, "though I'm not sure if there's anything good about it."

"I know . . . ," said Shiny, "the challenges have grown very large. But now you know a little more about the paths of water and all the life that depends on them. Not only the water you drink but every drop, salty or sweet. Now, you see that water can be ruined, and its ability to support life can be lost. So, you know that you must take care of it, as it is not something that will simply come out of the faucet forever."

Alex looked up and saw Bufflehead and a butterfly, both flapping their wings and hovering in place. Then Bufflehead quacked at Shiny and flew away.

Shiny and Alex walked in silence in the direction Bufflehead had gone, down the beach and around the distant peninsula.

Alex had much on her mind, and Shiny was right—she had just begun the journey, and now had more questions than when they had started. "Yes, I now know a little something more than I did before," she said slowly, "but tell me . . . what can I do about these big things you've shown me? It's all way too much for a kid to change."

Shiny gently placed his hand on the top of Alex's head. "Do you remember what I said about taking one step in the right direction?"

She recited: "One smart step, and the next will come much easier. But it hardly seems easy, and it seems too late."

"That's not the way to look at it," said Shiny. "We have to start somewhere, and somewhere is the spot where you are standing right now. We knew that my visit would be short, and so is the time people have to make changes. There is no time to waste, as change must start this very second. I will live the rest of my life as a whale, so my part in changing the future was to show you what was happening in the world around you. The responsibility for a better future is in the hands of kids like you. Children are the ones who can truly help our world . . . from water bugs to whales."

This made Alex think of a little girl from her neighborhood who spent lots of time gingerly walking the water's edge, looking for sea creatures in the tidepools, and rescuing those stranded on dry land. Alex imagined her saving a baby killer whale stuck on the beach, hoisting him up with superhuman strength and pushing him back into the water. And although some sadness still lingered in her heart, the image in her mind was funny, and it made her laugh. But the image vanished when Bufflehead appeared suddenly. He was quacking crazily, swooping toward them, and beating his wings in a furious blur of feathers.

Shiny's jaw dropped. He began to run, and Alex followed. And when they rounded the next peninsula, they saw a whale, not far from shore, struggling in a fisherman's nets. Alex waited for Shiny to act. But he just stared in shock as tears rolled down his cheeks. "It's my mother."

Alex was overtaken by a feeling of hopelessness, but then she saw something in the distance. "Look!" she shouted. "That's my father. There! Just down the shore! He can help!"

That day Alex covered the distance to her father as quickly as the little brown lizards that darted across the rocks in front of her house. And when Alex's father saw the look in his daughter's eyes, he leaped into action, launching his boat and speeding out to Shiny's mother.

Once there, he saw that the nets entangling her tail were pulling her down, so that only her head occasionally breached the surface for air. He shouted instructions to other nearby fishermen, and together they began slowly maneuvering their boats around the mother whale. With teamwork and care, they cautiously and patiently cut the nets away, and after many long minutes she was free.

Shiny's mother rose out of the water, landed with an enormous splash, and disappeared. But Shiny knew she was out there just below the surface, waiting for his return. He knew that his visit was near its end.

# CHAPTER 9

T he day after Alex's people saved Shiny's mother was the day he would return to the sea and be a whale again . . . a day that had come too soon for the little sister and brother.

As the sun set that evening, Alex and Shiny walked back down to the shore. Alex's father and mother went part of the way too, but they stopped to let the children reach the water's edge together.

"Listen and remember." Shiny held Alex's hand. "The things I showed you feel big and terrible, but there are simple lessons within them. The right way to live with our planet has been known by your people since the beginning. But as I said before, these truths are remembered and forgotten, remembered and forgotten. So now, it is your time to help people remember again."

The expression in Alex's dark eyes was grave and determined as she nodded and listened closely to Shiny's words.

"The pathways of water often change, but they always find the best direction," he said. "And so it will be when you do the right thing and others see your example. Change begins from that point on, much like the way your actions brought your people together to save my mother from the nets. Always try your best, as your best is what this world needs, and you are perfect for the task at hand. Now, tell me, Little Sister, what have you learned?"

Alex no longer felt the hopelessness of the day before. Her answer came quickly, and her sharp mind organized her thoughts into a rhyme, the way she had heard Shiny do.

> *Live in a good way with the world at large*
> *and take on each challenge no matter how hard.*
> *Each positive step, no matter how small,*
> *is the beginning of things getting better for all.*
> *With others I'll share all the truths that I learn,*
> *to help positive change come from each person in turn.*

Shiny grinned broadly, and the starlight from above reflected in his eyes. "Yes," he beamed. "Never lose hope, and remain the way you were born—strong, kind, and happy." And at that, Shiny gave Alex a long hug. Then he moved out into the water, wading in up to his knees.

"One more thing . . . ," Alex called from the beach, trying to delay Shiny's departure. "How did you know the places to travel here on land . . . so far from your world underwater?"

Shiny pointed to where Bufflehead sat preening his feathers on the beach. "You know the answer to that, Alex. It was from him. Bufflehead helped point the way."

"I know he's special," said Alex. "But it all sounded like duck noises to me. Just a whole lot of quacking and squawking." She smiled as she said this, her doubts and disbelief from earlier days replaced by all the real possibilities that dwell within the unexpected.

"Just keep listening," implored Shiny. "Pay close attention to the little things. There is still magic all around you."

Now the water was up to Shiny's waist. "Wait . . . ," pleaded Alex, "I don't want you to go. If you can't stay forever, then maybe just a little while longer?"

When Shiny called back to her, his voice sounded distant, as his words blended within the rhythm of the waves on the shore break. "The reason for my visit was to help you remember things that you've always carried inside of you. And now you are on a new path. Don't miss me, as I am a part of you, and you are a part of me, always. I will still be here in the world we share, and I will always be there in your heart. Maybe close . . . maybe far . . . but always there. Look out at the water when you stand on the beach. If you can't see me then, know I am there just beneath."

Alex put her hand over her heart and nodded. "Okay. I will look, listen, and remember. We are all family, and we are not letting go."

Now the water was up to Shiny's shoulders, and he called back to Alex one last time. "Whenever I'm close, I'll rise up out of the water so you will know that it's me." Then his head disappeared, like a seal dunking down to chase a quick-moving school of little silver fish.

"Keep watching, Alex," said a new voice. "See what happens next and do not be sad."

The voice startled her, but joy brightened her eyes when she turned to see Bufflehead down by her feet, looking out toward the waves.

"It's you!" cried Alex. "I knew it all along."

"Just keep looking," said the little duck.

And as Alex and Bufflehead watched side by side, the water swirled in a great shimmering whirlpool where Shiny had gone under. Where the surface had first appeared black, the glowing biolumines-cent lights grew so bright within the churning current that Alex could see the green of the ocean as the brilliant form of the water spirit rose from the deep. The spirit's long arm of seawater and starlight reached out toward the shore, toward Alex, and it touched her lightly on the head. And when the spirit receded back into the sea, Alex could feel the strength of the ocean within each beat of her heart, and she knew

this feeling would remain strong within her for the many days and seasons to come.

Then, as Alex and Bufflehead stared out toward the horizon, Shiny's mother surfaced in the distance to greet her child, just as the black fluke of a young whale rose from the water. It paused there for a moment, then slapped down hard against the waves with a sound that traveled far back into the forest. Shiny was home.

# CHAPTER 10

Months went by after Shiny's return to the ocean. Alex had not seen Bufflehead since, and although she felt the warmth and presence of Shiny within every heartbeat, she often looked out over the water for a breaching whale, but saw nothing. She had begun studying the things she and Shiny saw on their adventures, spending lots of time in the little community library. She also made long treks along the beach and into the countryside, finding strength and peace within the dappled light of the forest.

The journey with Shiny had opened the door to knowledge and the responsibility to act on it. With summer reaching its end, Alex walked through that doorway. At community gatherings she had seen adults get up and speak of important things. So despite being just a little kid, she gathered together as many of the children as she could.

The kids who showed up sat on logs down at the beach, just below Alex's thinking tree.

They stared at her as she scanned the horizon out over the ocean, getting her thoughts together. Then, she finally spoke. "As you all know, since our beginnings, our people have passed on knowledge by the oral tradition. We stand up and address the whole community when we have things that must be said . . . things that must be remembered. And kids, I have something very important to tell you. The world we are inheriting depends on it."

Alex was bursting with so much information . . . such overwhelming facts, feelings, and foretelling that for a moment she got stuck, and self-doubt got her tongue-tied. Then she heard a sound so faint and distant that she was unsure if it was real or imagined. But as it grew just slightly louder, she realized what it was . . . a whale song, drifting in from the ocean. The other kids took no notice and continued to stare at her expectantly.

Alex's vision blurred through a film of tears, and far off toward the horizon a whale's back appeared, just barely, followed by Shiny's tail rising and crashing to the surface, so far off that the sound didn't reach the children. Alex's courage grew, as the happiness over Shiny's presence filled her spirit. She felt the power of her voice return with the truth that it would carry, and then, in the blue sky before her, a small speck appeared. She wiped her eyes with the back of her hand, watching as the shape grew larger.

Bufflehead flew in from the distance. He made one turn around Alex, wheeling skillfully on his short wings, and dropped to the sand by her feet. All the children gasped in amazement. "Oh my gosh, look at that!" said Bella Bee, a five-year-old who caught the bus for kindergarten every day on the road behind Alex's house. "What the . . . ?"

Alex took a deep breath, grinning broadly. "Ignore Bufflehead for a second, Bella, and stay focused." Then, in a clear and confident voice, Alex said, "First, I have a very simple and straightforward thought for you all. When was the last time you could safely drink water from the rivers and streams of our land?"

"Never in our lifetime," said a neighbor boy. "You can't drink from any of the rivers here . . . not without getting sicker than little Gumby Anderson, who's home now in bed with the flu and an ice pack on her head."

"Right," said Alex. "Can't drink from the river without getting sicker than little Gumby Anderson. Now, think about it. That water has been flowing here since forever, for humans and all other animals to drink. So what could be more wrong than that? It is a sign, I tell you. One of countless signs from nature."

"We drink water from right out of the faucet," said another little girl, who was a couple years older than Alex and had doubts about giving her time to this pip-squeak.

At this Alex grinned. "I used to say the same thing," she acknowledged. "One of the reasons we cannot drink from rivers and streams is right there." She pointed to the smokestacks of the factory, the way Shiny had done months ago. "Listen and remember. I'm going to tell you about my amazing experiences of this last summer, and how I learned that water is the foundation of life . . . how I saw that all life is connected. Every animal . . . you, me, whales, ducks, and any other creature you can name, must have water to survive." Now Alex glanced down at Bufflehead then back to the kids.

"And every animal . . . every living creature depends on the existence of the creatures around it to survive. So, without water there is no life. I don't want you to just hear my words. I need you to truly see what is happening in the world right now, as humans disrupt the paths of water . . . as humans disrupt the natural order that is sustained by water."

Alex looked at her audience and in some of the faces she recognized the dread that she herself had felt not long ago.

"I'm going to tell you difficult truths about what is happening to our world. These things I share will only scratch the surface, but the path of learning goes on forever, and following that path is up to you. And I know that when you see the truth of what is happening to our earth, you will fight for the environment that keeps us alive. For the health of our future, it is your voices that matter the most, and we will do this together . . . one small step in the right direction. One smart step at a time."

Alex made sure she was ready for bed early that night because she'd promised the kids that the next morning she would lead them on an exploration through the countryside and up into the foothills. Shortly after the sun went down, Alex was sleeping soundly in her little village by the shore. And she dreamed of helping all the world's creatures, from water bugs to whales.

# Glossary of Environmental Terms

**Aquatic organisms:** living things that live in bodies of water.

**Arctic:** located near the north pole, a cold region that is covered in ice.

**Baleen:** a bristly plate within a whale's mouth that helps filter out food sources, like krill, from sea water.

**Bioluminescence:** light created by living creatures, like algae and certain fish. Phosphorescence is light emitted without heat.

**Climate change:** a naturally occurring temperature rise that occurs on earth. However, human pollution is accelerating climate change rapidly.

**Coast Salish:** Native or Indigenous peoples that are from the Pacific Northwest.

**Coral bleaching:** the dying of coral reef ecosystems as a result of harmful pollution.

**Coral reef:** marine limestone that is made up of tiny organisms.

**Currents:** the water flows of lakes, rivers, and other bodies of water.

**Ecosystem:** a community of species that help each other survive and thrive as a unit.

**Environmental justice:** environmental challenges and impacts affecting the health and sustainability of communities, particularly for future generations, regardless of race, class, gender, and other identities. Challenges result from threats to natural resources due to human actions and influences.

**Fin:** the top or bottom portion of fish or marine mammals that have a fish shape. These are the body parts that help them maneuver in the water and swim efficiently.

**Food webs:** the tiers of food that each organism or species consumes.

**Forest:** an ecosystem that is made up of a lot of trees and underbrush.

**Glaciers:** large bodies of ice that make up regions like the arctic.

**Krill:** shrimp or crustaceans that also make up the main character's diet—his main food source.

**Lakes:** bodies of water that are surrounded by soil and land. The water can be salt water or fresh water.

**Marine debris:** pollution that consists of pieces of plastic, fishing nets, and more, often found in the oceans.

**Marshes:** wetland ecosystems that do not include trees and usually consist of soft soil such as mud.

**Ocean:** covers the majority of the earth (three-fourths) and consists of salt water.

**Orca:** also known as killer whales. Not related to whales but rather to dolphins. They are predatory and hunt in packs. Many Arctic peoples refer to them as "sea wolves."

**Plankton:** small organisms that are usually algae or protozoa. One of the main food sources of the main character—a whale.

**Pollution:** harmful substances, such as exhaust from cars, introduced into the environment. Usually caused by humans.

**Polynesian:** Indigenous peoples from the South Pacific Islands.

**Ponds:** bodies of water that are also surrounded by soil and land. Ponds are smaller than lakes and are sometimes artificial.

**Seaweed:** algae that grow in water, usually salt water. They are marine plants that play a big role in the carbon cycle.

**Trenches:** in the oceans, trenches are naturally occurring big holes and excavations.

**Walrus:** a large marine mammal that is related to seals. It usually has long tusks.

**Waves:** movement of ocean waters or any other body of water that results in angled positions.

**Whale:** a large marine mammal that belongs to the cetacean family. The main species or animal of this story.

# Student Resources

## Pacific Northwest Native Cultures

Where is the Pacific Northwest? Have students think-pair-share. They can mention their guesses to a fellow classmate and then share their guesses with the entire class.

The Pacific Northwest extends from Northern California to the southern coast of Alaska. This region includes Washington, Oregon, Northern California, and British Columbia, Canada. When discussing regions, it is important to learn about the Indigenous peoples of those lands, especially given the context of this book. Indigenous peoples are still here and continue to hold a strong relationship with their traditional homelands—as for generations their ancestors have lived and carried on their rich cultures and ways of life in those lands. We can view their strong kinships with our environment in *The Whale Child*. Acknowledging the original peoples of those lands is an important practice, as Indigenous peoples are often ignored or silenced. This is also known as **land acknowledgment**.

Land acknowledgment is when the original peoples of those lands—Indigenous peoples—are recognized before a talk, presentation, etc. takes place. For example, if we were giving a presentation in Seattle, we would do a land acknowledgment as follows: "We would like to acknowledge the original people of this land—the Duwamish people, whose traditional homelands we are upon." This is a classroom activity teachers can start implementing in their classes before each session. It allows students to become more aware of the Indigenous peoples that still reside in their cities, counties, and states.

In the Pacific Northwest, Indigenous peoples are recognized as sovereign nations, as are all federally recognized tribes throughout the US. They are also known as tribes, tribal nations, and First Nations. Each tribe has a democratically elected self-governing body or tribal council, which consists of a tribal chairperson and other members. The political structure of each tribe is different and unique to their respective cultural practices and community needs. Since *The Whale Child* focuses on the Coast Salish people, and the story takes place in Washington, we will focus on the tribes of this state.

The state of Washington has twenty-nine federally recognized tribes, which are listed in the table below. We have included a student project idea to further discuss the tribes of Washington and increase knowledge and awareness in your classroom.

**WASHINGTON STATE TRIBES**

| | | | |
|---|---|---|---|
| Chehalis | Makah | Quinault | Squaxin Island |
| Colville | Muckleshoot | Samish | Stillaguamish |
| Cowlitz | Nisqually | Sauk-Suiattle | Suquamish |
| Hoh | Nooksack | Shoalwater | Swinomish |
| Jamestown | Port Gamble | Skokomish | Tulalip |
| Kalispel | Puyallup | Snoqualmie | Upper Skagit |
| Lower Elwha | Quileute | Spokane | Yakama |
| Lummi | | | |

## Student Project: Poster Presentation

Have students choose one of the twenty-nine federally recognized tribes listed in the preceding table and complete a poster to present in class. These posters can create a classroom archive for future lessons. The poster must include the following information:

- 1–2 historical facts of the tribe selected

- 1–2 cultural facts of the tribe selected

- 3–4 traditional foods of the people from each tribe selected

- The location of the tribe

- 1–2 interesting facts you found while researching additional information about the tribe

- 4–5 pictures of each tribe

### *Teacher Suggestions*

1. You can adapt the project to incorporate technology. Students can create their poster utilizing programs such as PowerPoint. Presenting their poster to the class allows them to work on their presentation skills.

2. You can also change the focus from Washington State tribes to the entire Pacific Northwest (which includes the southern coast of Alaska; British Columbia, Canada; Northern California; and Oregon). This will allow students to increase their knowledge of and expertise on geography. It will also help students begin to learn about the history, contributions, and cultures of our country's

First Nations peoples. This is a good suggestion for classes that have more than twenty-nine students.

3. Pair students: If you think it is best for your class to enhance their collaborative and teamwork skills, they can complete this project in pairs or in groups.

# Coast Salish People: Known as the People of the Cedar

The Coast Salish people are Indigenous to the Pacific Northwest Coast from the Columbia River in Oregon to British Columbia, Canada. Archaeological evidence demonstrates that the Coast Salish people have resided in the Pacific Northwest since 9000 BCE. Currently, there are an estimated 56,000 Coast Salish people residing in the United States and Canada.

The cedar tree, known to many Indigenous peoples as the "long-life maker," has always held an essential and sacred place in the life of Coast Salish people. For thousands of years, the generosity of the cedar tree has given the Coast Salish people the means to create their clothing, build their longhouses and canoes, carve their ceremonial masks, and more. To this day, the people honor the generous spirit of cedar and never harvest from the tree without first making an offering of gratitude. This exemplifies the teaching that we must respect and care for the living gifts we receive from the natural world.

After an offering is made, cedar bark is harvested by peeling the inner and outer bark from a living tree. When done correctly, this does not harm the tree. Traditional Coast Salish clothing was made from the inner bark of cedar trees, which naturally repels the rain.

Coast Salish cedar weaving is an elaborate art form that often integrates intricate patterns and designs that are seen as gifts from the ancestors and nature. These designs are often woven into regalia and basketry. Some baskets are woven so tightly that the people are able to boil water in them. Many Coast Salish people still use cedar baskets for gathering foods and medicines, while others are used as fine art. Each piece carries the spirit of the cedar and the good thoughts, respect, and knowledge of the weaver.

Fishing is a way of life for the Coast Salish people. As a result, the Salish Sea is an important cultural region where they continue to fish salmon for sustenance. Their traditional diets consist of salmon, shellfish, duck, deer, elk, huckleberries, nettle, wild onion, wild celery, and much more. Some of the tribes used to rely on whale meat before whaling was banned in both the United States and Canada. Other plant and animal species native to the Pacific Northwest also make up part of their traditional diet. *We have included a project for your students to allow you to discuss traditional foods and food sovereignty with them.*

Traditional Coast Salish houses included longhouses, also known as plank houses. A lot of longhouses were burned down or removed by European settlers during the time of colonization. Many Indigenous spiritual and cultural practices were prohibited and punishable by law until August 11, 1978, when the Native American Religious Freedom Act was passed. After centuries of oppression, Indigenous peoples of the US were legally able to practice their ancestral ways of life for the first time.

In the longhouses, they hosted a **potlatch,** which in the Chinook language means "gifting." Potlatches took days and weeks and were traditional gatherings for various reasons: to bestow or transfer names and rights, to validate marriages, to recognize youth's coming of age, and to mourn and honor the dead. They hold four functions: political, economic, social, and ceremonial or spiritual. The guests were seated according to their ranking or status. Unfortunately, due to the government's assimilation policies, there was a ban on potlatches from 1884 to 1951. Those caught having a potlatch were sent to jail or were forced to pay a hefty price. However, some Coast Salish people held secret potlatches, but fear of arrest and imprisonment was always present.

Coast Salish people are also known for their advanced technology. This advanced technology allowed them to build canoes that were engineered to navigate the strong winds and waves of the Salish Sea. The canoe traditions are kept alive through **canoe journeys**—annual journeys where families gather and paddle to the tribe that is hosting the canoe journey that year. Each canoe is represented by a canoe family.

Coast Salish people have maintained their culture despite the oppressive colonial systems they have always faced. A short video that can be shown to the class is titled *Teachings of the Tree People: The Work of Bruce Miller* (https://vimeo.com/64099709).

You can have students watch an artistic production titled "People of the Salish Sea (Coast Salish)" from the film *Clearwater* (www.youtube.com/watch?v=2tQMZttQV0w).

## Student Project: Traditional Foods

Have students draw a traditional foods plate. Traditional foods refer to cultural foods that hold significance in their families or are recipes passed down to them. This will allow students to explore the role traditional foods have in their cultures and families. Some discussion questions they can answer are:

1. What traditional foods did you draw?

2. How often do you eat these traditional foods?

3. Who usually cooks them?

4. Is it hard to purchase these foods or the ingredients at the store?

5. Where do you purchase these foods or ingredients?

6. Where do these traditional foods come from?

# ENVIRONMENTAL CHALLENGES

It is important to note that Indigenous cultures, which include aspects like foods, stories, languages, songs, and so on, are the result of a harmonious relationship with the natural world, cultivated over millennia. When the local environment is subjected to degradation, ways of life are directly and negatively impacted. Coast Salish people face many environmental threats and challenges in their regions, and they have united with peoples of diverse communities to stand up for environmental justice. The definition of environmental justice may vary from place to place in accordance with the regional priorities for protecting the health and sustainability of homelands for future generations. For the Coast Salish people, environmental justice encompasses the following:

1. Protection of natural resources

2. Climate change adaptation and mitigation

3. Increasing awareness of the environmental challenges they face

4. Addressing equity

5. Community responsibility

6. Creating sustainable solutions

7. Becoming proactive

8. Having equal access to natural resources

9. Giving a voice to silenced or ignored communities, human and nonhuman

10. Replenishing sustainable resources

11. Passing natural resources protection laws

Environmental justice and the challenges Indigenous communities in the Pacific Northwest face cannot be discussed without mentioning the treaties. The United States government signed more than five hundred treaties with the Indigenous nations acknowledging their sovereign status. A treaty is an agreement between two nations—in this case the tribe and the United States. Treaties are like the US Constitution—supreme laws that cannot be broken by any entities. However, in the state of Washington, treaties were not enforced or respected by the government until the **Fish Wars** occurred. The Fish Wars were known as the civil rights movement led by Indigenous people in the state of Washington, for which they also received support from the African American community. They were an act of peaceful protest against the inactive protocol and enforcement of the Stevens Treaties signed in 1854 and 1855 by the twenty-nine federally recognized tribes of the state of Washington. These treaties gave Native peoples the right to fish, hunt, and gather in their "usual and accustomed" territories. However, the state of Washington was not enforcing these treaties, and, as a result, the Indigenous communities fought for this right. The fish-ins started in the 1960s, and in 1974, this case was

brought to court. Judge Boldt was the lead judge in this case, and after he interpreted the law, he decided that the tribes did have the right to take 50 percent of the harvestable fish and had the right to fish in their accustomed areas. This historical decision is known as the Boldt Decision, which finally reacknowledged the right of tribes to fish their usual and accustomed areas again—a right that was originally outlined in the treaties, but not respected. Fish plays a major role in their culture and is a main staple of their traditional foods to this day.

However, despite the Boldt Decision, environmental challenges continue to impact the Washington State tribes. This is due to climate change and how it is exacerbating environmental degradation. Climate change in combination with human-made pollution is impacting reservations and traditional lands in the state of Washington. For instance, pipelines have become a constant threat to the Washington State tribes as they are routed through their reservations. Another example of environmental challenges are proposed coal terminals in Washington State. In 2011, Pacific International Terminals proposed the Gateway Pacific Terminal at Cherry Point in Whatcom County, Washington. Cherry Point is known as Xwe'chi'eXen by the Lummi Nation. For more than 175 generations, it was a Lummi ancestral village of great significance. Fortunately for the salmon, the whales, and all inhabitants of the Salish Sea, in 2016 the Lummi Nation worked with other tribes and environmental organizations to defeat this proposal, citing the Lummi Nation's treaty fishing rights, which date back to 1855.

Other environmental challenges that impact the Washington State tribes include deforestation, invasive species outcompeting native species, overfishing, overharvesting native plants, ocean acidification, dams, oil drilling, and more.

# Common Core Questions: Classroom Discussion— Grades 3, 4, and 5

~~~~~~~~~~~~~~~~~~~~~~~~~~~~~~~~~~~~~~~~~~~~~~

### Question 1

*Based on the reading and the overall message of the story, what do you think "timeless songs that carry the stories and wisdom of life on earth" refers to or signifies?*

**Grade 3—Common Core Standard:** CCSS.ELA-LITERACY.RL.3.2 Recount stories, including fables, folktales, and myths from diverse cultures; determine the central message, lesson, or moral and explain how it is conveyed through key details in the text.

**Grade 4—Common Core Standard:** CCSS.ELA-LITERACY.W.4.1.A
Introduce a topic or text clearly, state an opinion, and create an organizational structure in which related ideas are grouped to support the writer's purpose.

**Grade 5—Common Core Standard:** CCSS.ELA-LITERACY.RL.5.2
Determine a theme of a story, drama, or poem from details in the text, including how characters in a story or drama respond to challenges or how the speaker in a poem reflects upon a topic; summarize the text.

## Question 2

*What is happening to the health of the ocean? How are humans responsible? What are Shiny's opinions in regard to this issue?*

**Grade 3—Common Core Standard:** CCSS.ELA-LITERACY.RI.3.5
Use text features and search tools (such as keywords, sidebars, and hyperlinks) to locate information relevant to a given topic efficiently.

**Grade 4—Common Core Standard:** CCSS.ELA-LITERACY.RI.4.3
Explain events, procedures, ideas, or concepts in a historical, scientific, or technical text, including what happened and why, based on specific information in the text.

**Grade 5—Common Core Standard:** CCSS.ELA-LITERACY.RI.5.2
Determine two or more main ideas of a text and explain how they are supported by key details; summarize the text.

## Question 3

*How are pieces of plastic, nets, and plastic soda pop rings impacting fish and birds? What scene does Alex witness that shows how they are impacting the fish and birds?*

**Grade 3—Common Core Standard:** CCSS.ELA-LITERACY.RL.3.5

Refer to parts of stories, dramas, and poems when writing or speaking about a text, using terms such as *chapter, scene,* and *stanza;* describe how each successive part builds on earlier sections.

**Grade 4—Common Core Standard:** CCSS.ELA-LITERACY.W.4.2.B

Develop the topic with facts, definitions, concrete details, quotations, or other information and examples related to the topic.

**Grade 5—Common Core Standard:** CCSS.ELA-LITERACY.RI.5.1
Quote accurately from a text when explaining what the text says explicitly and when drawing inferences from the text.

## Question 4

*Describe the first encounter Alex had with Shiny. What did Alex learn from her mother in regard to where Shiny came from?*

**Grade 3—Common Core Standard:** CCSS.ELA-LITERACY.RF.3.4.A
Read grade-level text with purpose and understanding.

**Grade 4—Common Core Standard:** CCSS.ELA-LITERACY.RF.4.4.A
Read grade-level text with purpose and understanding.

**Grade 5—Common Core Standard:** CCSS.ELA-LITERACY.RF.5.4.A
Read grade-level text with purpose and understanding.

## Question 5

*According to Shiny, how do farms and factories harm the soil and rivers?*

**Grade 3—Common Core Standard:** CCSS.ELA-LITERACY.RI.3.3
Describe the relationship between a series of historical events, scientific ideas or concepts, or steps in technical procedures in a text, using language that pertains to time, sequence, and cause and effect.

**Grade 4—Common Core Standard:** CCSS.ELA-LITERACY.RI.4.5
Describe the overall structure (such as chronology, comparison, cause and effect, problem and solution) of events, ideas, concepts, or information in a text or part of a text.

**Grade 5—Common Core Standard:** CCSS.ELA-LITERACY.RI.5.5
Compare and contrast the overall structure (such as chronology, comparison, cause and effect, problem and solution) of events, ideas, concepts, or information in two or more texts.

## Question 6

*In your opinion, what is the most important lesson Alex learns from Shiny? Do you agree this is an important lesson to teach other children? Why or why not?*

**Grade 3—Common Core Standard:** CCSS.ELA-LITERACY.RF.3.4.C
Use context to confirm or self-correct word recognition and understanding, rereading as necessary.

**Grade 4—Common Core Standard:** CCSS.ELA-LITERACY.RF.4.4.B
Read grade-level prose and poetry orally with accuracy, appropriate rate, and expression on successive readings.

**Grade 5—Common Core Standard:** CCSS.ELA-LITERACY.RF.5.4.C
Use context to confirm or self-correct word recognition and under-standing, rereading as necessary.

## Question 7

*Shiny teaches Alex about the water cycle throughout their walk.*
*Describe and draw the water cycle.*

**Grade 3—Common Core Standard:** CCSS.ELA-LITERACY.SL.3.1.C
Ask questions to check understanding of the information presented, stay on topic, and link their comments to the remarks of others.

**Grade 4—Common Core Standard:** CCSS.ELA-LITERACY.SL.4.1.C
Pose and respond to specific questions to clarify or follow up on infor-mation, and make comments that contribute to the discussion and link to the remarks of others.

**Grade 5—Common Core Standard:** CCSS.ELA-LITERACY.SL.5.2
Summarize a written text read aloud or information presented in diverse media and formats, including visually, quantitatively, and orally.

# Question 8

*What is the significance of water to you? How does this compare to what water signifies to Shiny?*

**Grade 3—Common Core Standard:** CCSS.ELA-LITERACY.SL.3.4

Report on a topic or text, tell a story, or recount an experience with appropriate facts and relevant, descriptive details, speaking clearly at an understandable pace.

**Grade 4—Common Core Standard:** CCSS.ELA-LITERACY.SL.4.4
Report on a topic or text, tell a story, or recount an experience in an organized manner, using appropriate facts and relevant, descriptive details to support main ideas or themes; speak clearly at an understandable pace.

**Grade 5—Common Core Standard:** CCSS.ELA-LITERACY.SL.5.4
Report on a topic or text or present an opinion, sequencing ideas logically and using appropriate facts and relevant, descriptive details to support main ideas or themes; speak clearly at an understandable pace.

## Question 9

*Alex recalls an important lesson passed down to her from her relatives: "Take only what you need from nature; waste nothing, and give thanks for what you take." What does this mean?*

**Grade 3—Common Core Standard:** CCSS.ELA-LITERACY.SL.3.3
Ask and answer questions about information from a speaker, offering appropriate elaboration and detail.

**Grade 4—Common Core Standard:** CCSS.ELA-LITERACY.SL.4.3
Identify the reasons and evidence a speaker provides to support particular points.

**Grade 5—Common Core Standard:** CCSS.ELA-LITERACY.SL.5.3
Summarize the points a speaker makes and explain how each claim is supported by reasons and evidence.

## Question 10

*In chapter 8, Shiny gets to see his mother. What is happening to her? How did she end up in this scenario?*

**Grade 3—Common Core Standard:** CCSS.ELA-LITERACY.RL.3.5
Refer to parts of stories, dramas, and poems when writing or speaking

about a text, using terms such as *chapter, scene,* and *stanza;* describe how each successive part builds on earlier sections.

**Grade 4—Common Core Standard:** CCSS.ELA-LITERACY.W.4.2.B
Develop the topic with facts, definitions, concrete details, quotations, or other information and examples related to the topic.

**Grade 5—Common Core Standard:** CCSS.ELA-LITERACY.RI.5.1
Quote accurately from a text when explaining what the text says explicitly and when drawing inferences from the text.

## Question 11

*Do you agree with Alex's statement regarding everything she witnessed and learned from Shiny, "What can I do about these big things you've shown me? It's all way too much for a kid to change." Why or why not? Can kids change these things?*

**Grade 3—Common Core Standard:** CCSS.ELA-LITERACY.SL.3.3
Ask and answer questions about information from a speaker, offering appropriate elaboration and detail.

**Grade 4—Common Core Standard:** CCSS.ELA-LITERACY.SL.4.3
Identify the reasons and evidence a speaker provides to support particular points.

**Grade 5—Common Core Standard:** CCSS.ELA-LITERACY.SL.5.3
Summarize the points a speaker makes and explain how each claim is supported by reasons and evidence.

# Resources

## Online

American Museum of Natural History. "Coast Salish." https://tinyurl
.com/y4n9vdd8.

James, Bill. 2014. "Lummi Nation's Fight Against a Coal Terminal."
August 11, 2014. Video, 2:42. https://vimeo.com/103149296.

Julius, Jay. 2013. "How Much Coal Will the Gateway Pacific Terminal
Bring?" Filmed June 11, 2013. Video, 3:35. https://vimeo.com
/69192861.

Schwartz, Ralph. 2015. "Lummi Nation Asks Army Corps to Reject
Cherry Point Coal Terminal." *Bellingham Herald,* January 5, 2015.
https://tinyurl.com/y5cblyd6.

Washington State Department of Social and Health Services. "Washington Tribes." https://tinyurl.com/y5uhb4zg.

White, Sophia. 2015. "A Very Short History of the Coast Salish People."
    *Culture Trip,* December 10, 2015. https://tinyurl.com/y2arcrf8.
Wilbur, Matika, dir. 2015. "Stop Coal Exports: Protect Cherry Point." October 19, 2015. Video, 3:19. www.youtube.com/watch?v=-0SLA7VUkvo.

## Journals

Hernandez, Jessica, and Kristiina Vogt. 2017. "Environmental Justice
    in the Pacific Northwest: Developing an Atlas & Website to Identify
    Indigenous Pillars of Environmental Justice for Policy Recommendations." Seattle: University of Washington. www.jessicabhernandez
    .com/ejpnw.html.
U.S. Environmental Protection Agency, Office of Policy. 2015.
    "EJScreen: Environmental Justice Mapping and Screening Tool."
    https://tinyurl.com/y5xk8boy.
Velasquez, Alcides, and Robert LaRose. 2015. "Social Media for Social
    Change: Social Media Political Efficacy and Activism in Student
    Activist Groups." *Journal of Broadcasting & Electronic Media* 59
    (3): 456–74. https://doi.org/10.1080/08838151.2015.1054998.
Vickery, Jamie, and Lori M. Hunter. 2016. "Native Americans: Where
    in Environmental Justice Research?" *Society & Natural Resources*
    29 (1): 36–52. https://doi.org/10.1080/08941920.2015.1045644.

# ACKNOWLEDGMENTS

We would like to thank the staff at North Atlantic Books for their dedication and the supportive, enjoyable working relationship they inspired. Special thanks to our friend Mateo Gamlen for his insight, expertise, and help with bringing the visual concept of our story to life.

# About the Authors

KEITH T. A. EGAWA is a novelist who focuses on both adult and children's literature. He is a Washington native and a member of the Lummi Indian Nation. Egawa's extensive experience in the field of child welfare has provided him with both inspiration and insight into his subject matter.

CHENOA T. Y. EGAWA is Coast Salish of the Lummi and S'Klallam Nations of Washington State. She is a medicine woman, singer, writer, illustrator, photographer, and teacher dedicated to bringing healing to our Mother Earth and to people of all origins. She is a voice to bring Native wisdom and perspectives to the world when these teachings are particularly poignant reminders of our shared responsibility to live with respect for ourselves, one another, and all that gives us life.

Special thanks to Jessica Hernandez, who contributed material for the glossary, educational passages, and common core discussion questions. She is an Indigenous environmental scientist, conservationist, and artisan. She advocates for the inclusion of Indigenous and Black communities through the integration of decolonial, feminist, and environmental, climate, and food justice principles, with the belief that uplifting these communities can help address environmental sustainability and conservation effectively. She is the founder of Piña Soul SPC, which supports environmental sustainability and conservation among Black and Indigenous communities.